THE NIGHT BEFORE CHRISTMAS

A Family Treasury of Songs, Poems, and Stories

When Friends Drop In, 1961

Illustrations by
Haddon H. Sundblom

 Publications International, Ltd.

Front cover art: *For Santa, 1950*
Back cover art: *The Pause That Refreshes, 1958*

Published by
Louis Weber, C.E.O.
Publications International, Ltd.
7373 North Cicero Avenue
Lincolnwood, Illinois 60712

Ground Floor, 59 Gloucester Place
London W1U 8JJ

Customer Service: 1-800-595-8484 or customer_service@pilbooks.com

8 7 6 5 4 3 2 1

ISBN-13: 978-1-4127-6752-1
ISBN-10: 1-4127-6752-0

TABLE OF CONTENTS

A Visit From St. Nicholas

Written by Clement Clarke Moore

'Twas the night before Christmas, when all through the house,

 Not a creature was stirring, not even a mouse.

The stockings were hung by the chimney with care,

 In hopes that St. Nicholas soon would be there.

The children were nestled all snug in their beds,

 While visions of sugarplums danced in their heads.

And Mamma in her kerchief, and I in my cap,

 Had just settled down for a long winter's nap.

When out on the lawn there arose such a clatter,

 I sprang from the bed to see what was the matter.

Away to the window I flew like a flash,

 Tore open the shutter and threw up the sash.

The moon on the breast of the new-fallen snow

 Gave the lustre of midday to objects below.

When what to my wondering eyes should appear

 But a miniature sleigh and eight tiny reindeer.

Santa Please Pause Here, 1963

With a little old driver, so lively and quick,

I knew in a moment it must be St. Nick!

More rapid than eagles, his coursers they came,

And he whistled, and shouted, and called them by name.

"Now, Dasher!

Now, Dancer!

Now, Prancer and Vixen!

On, Comet!
On, Cupid!
On, Donner and Blitzen!

To the top of the porch, to the top of the wall,

Now, dash away, dash away, dash away all!"

As dry leaves that before the wild hurricane fly,

When they meet with an obstacle, mount to the sky,

So up to the housetop the coursers they flew,

With the sleigh full of toys and St. Nicholas, too.

And then, in a twinkling, I heard on the roof,

The prancing and pawing of each little hoof.

As I drew in my head, and was turning around,

Down the chimney St. Nicholas came with a bound.

He was dressed all in fur, from his head to his foot,

And his clothes were all tarnished with ashes and soot.

A bundle of toys he had flung on his back,

And he looked like a peddler just opening his sack.

His eyes, how they twinkled, his dimples, how merry!

His cheeks were like roses, his nose like a cherry.

His droll little mouth was drawn up like a bow,

And the beard of his chin was as white as the snow.

The stump of a pipe he held tight in his teeth,

And the smoke, it encircled his head like a wreath.

He had a broad face and a little round belly,

That shook when he laughed, **like a bowlful of** jelly.

He was chubby and plump, a right jolly old elf,

And I laughed when I saw him, in spite of myself.

A wink of his eye, and a twist of his head,

Soon gave me to know I had nothing to dread.

He spoke not a word, but went straight to his work,

And filled all the stockings, then turned with a jerk.

And laying his finger aside of his nose,

And giving a nod, up the chimney he rose.

He sprang to his sleigh, to his team gave a whistle,

And away they all flew like the down of a thistle.

But I heard him exclaim, as they drove out of sight,

"Happy Christmas to all, and to all a good night!"

Untitled, 1965

Jolly Old St. Nicholas

Traditional Carol

Jolly old St. Nicholas,
    Lean your ear this way.
Don't you tell a single soul
    What I'm going to say.
Christmas Eve is coming soon.
    Now you dear old man,
Whisper what you'll bring to me;
    Tell me if you can.

When the clock is striking twelve,
    When I'm fast asleep,
Down the chimney, broad and black,
    With your pack you'll creep.
All the stockings you will find
    Hanging in a row.
Mine will be the shortest one;
    You'll be sure to know.

Johnny wants a pair of skates.
    Susy wants a sled.
Nelly wants a picture book,
    Yellow, blue, and red.
Now I think I'll leave to you
    What to give the rest.
Choose for me, dear Santa Claus,
    You will know the best.

I Am the Christmas Spirit

From the poem by E. C. Baird

I am the Christmas Spirit!
  I cause the aged to renew their youth,
and to laugh in the old, glad way.
  I keep romance alive in the heart of childhood,
and brighten sleep with
    dreams woven of magic.

I cause eager feet to climb dark stairways
    with filled baskets,
leaving behind hearts amazed
    at the goodness of the world.

Yes, Virginia, There Is a Santa Claus

Long ago, in 1897, a young girl named Virginia O'Hanlon wrote a letter to her city's newspaper, *The Sun*. Virginia had a question and she hoped the newspaper would have the answer. It was an important question, and one that millions of curious children continue to ask today. Here is Virginia's thoughtful question, and the beloved answer that is still worth repeating.

Editorial Page, *New York Sun*, 1897

Written by Francis P. Church

We take pleasure in answering thus prominently the communication below, expressing at the same time our great gratification that its faithful author is numbered among the friends of *The Sun*:

Dear Editor,

I am 8 years old. Some of my friends say there is no Santa Claus. Papa says, "If you see it in *The Sun*, it's so." Please tell me the truth. Is there a Santa Claus?

Virginia O'Hanlon

Greetings, 1945

Virginia, your little friends are wrong. They do not believe except what they see.

Yes, Virginia, there is a Santa Claus. He exists as certainly as love and generosity and devotion exist, and you know that they abound and give to your life its highest beauty and joy. Alas! How dreary would be the world if there were no Santa Claus!

It would be as dreary as if there were no Virginias. There would be no childlike faith then, no poetry, no romance to make tolerable this existence. We should have no enjoyment, except in sense and sight. The external light with which childhood fills the world would be extinguished.

Not believe in Santa Claus! You might as well not believe in fairies. You might get your papa to hire men to watch in all the chimneys on Christmas Eve to catch Santa Claus, but even if you did not see Santa Claus coming down, what would that prove?

Nobody sees Santa Claus, but that is no sign that there is no Santa Claus. The most real things in the world are those that neither children nor men can see. Did you ever see fairies dancing on the lawn? Of course not, but that's no proof that they are not there.

Nobody can conceive or imagine all the wonders

that are unseen and unseeable in the world.

You tear apart the baby's rattle and see what makes the noise inside, but there is a veil covering the unseen world which not the strongest man, nor even the united strength of all the strongest men that ever lived could tear apart. Only faith, poetry, love, romance, can push aside that curtain and view and picture the supernal beauty and glory beyond. Is it all real? Ah, Virginia, in all this world there is nothing as real and abiding.

No Santa Claus? Thank God he lives and lives forever. A thousand years from now, Virginia, nay 10 times 10,000 years from now, he will continue to make glad the heart of childhood.

Up on the Housetop

Written by Benjamin R. Hanby

Up on the housetop reindeer pause;
    Out jumps good ol' Santa Claus!
Down through the chimney with lots of toys;
    All for the little ones' Christmas joys.

First comes the stocking of little Nell;
    Oh, dear Santa, fill it well.
Give her a dolly that laughs and cries,
    One that will open and shut her eyes.

Ho! Ho! Ho! Who wouldn't go?
    Ho! Ho! Ho! Who wouldn't go?
Up on the housetop, click, click, click!
    Down through the chimney with good Saint Nick.

Next comes the stocking of little Will;
    Oh, just see what a glorious fill.
Here is a hammer and plastic tacks,
    Also a ball and a game of jacks.

Ho! Ho! Ho! Who wouldn't go?
    Ho! Ho! Ho! Who wouldn't go?
Up on the housetop, click, click, click!
    Down through the chimney with good Saint Nick.

They Remembered Me, 1942

O Christmas Tree

Traditional German Carol

O Christmas tree, O Christmas tree,
　Your leaves are so unchanging.
O Christmas tree, O Christmas tree,
　Your leaves are so unchanging.
Not only green when summer glows,
　But in the winter when it snows.
O Christmas tree, O Christmas tree,
　Your leaves are so unchanging.

O Christmas tree, O Christmas tree,
　You fill our hearts with warm cheer.
O Christmas tree, O Christmas tree,
　You fill our hearts with warm cheer.
On Christmas Day you stand so tall,
　Affording joy to one and all.
O Christmas tree, O Christmas tree,
　You fill our hearts with warm cheer.
You fill our hearts with warm cheer.

Santa's List

Written by Carla Tarini

Each year I must consult my list
    To see who has been nice.
First I'll check through all the names,
    And then I'll check it twice.
I've got at least ten thousand Jacks
    And hundreds called René,
And dozens more named Sam and Grace
    Just in the USA!

Ah! Look at all these darling dears
    Who help their mommies out:
They sweep the floors and make their beds,
    And hardly ever shout.
Yet over here, the naughty ones,
    They dribble milk from straws.
(But, oops! I did the same last night
    For laughs with Mrs. Claus!)

'Cause naughty can be funny,
    You know fun is fine with me;
And even if it makes a mess
    It's no catastrophe.
Perhaps I'll move these naughty names —
    But do you think I should?
A toy for every girl and boy;
    All Santa's kids are good!

Good Boys and Girls, 1951

I'll Be Waiting for You, Santa

Written by Carla Tarini

I'll be waiting for you, Santa,
  Waiting right here by the tree.
I'll be curled up in the armchair,
  Dipping cookies in my tea.
I'll be reading stories, Santa,
  Reading tales of how you flew
Into wild and windy snowstorms,
  But each time you made it through.

I'll be thinking of you, Santa,
  Thinking of your silver sleigh
Filled with sparkle-papered presents
  To be opened Christmas Day.
I'll be listening for you, Santa,
  Listening for your hearty cheer
And the clip-clop on the rooftop
  Of your strong and dashing deer.

Refreshing Surprise, 1959

$\mathcal{I}$'ll be watching for you, Santa,

 Watching for your shiny boot,

As you slide down through the chimney

 In your holly-jolly suit.

I'll be waiting for you, Santa,

 Waiting right here by the tree.

But Santa, if I'm sleeping,

 Will you please awaken me?

We Wish You a Merry Christmas

Traditional Carol

We wish you a merry Christmas,
We wish you a merry Christmas,
We wish you a merry Christmas,
And a happy new year.

Good tidings we bring
To you and your kin,
Good tidings for Christmas
And a happy new year.

Now bring us some figgy pudding,
Now bring us some figgy pudding,
Now bring us some figgy pudding,
And a cup
of good cheer!

Hospitality, 1948

Deck the Halls

Traditional Carol

Deck the halls with boughs of holly, fa la la la la, la la la la.
'Tis the season to be jolly, fa la la la la, la la la la.
Don we now our gay apparel, fa la la, la la la, la la la.
Troll the ancient yuletide carol, fa la la la la, la la la la.

See the blazing yule before us, fa la la la la, la la la la.
Strike the harp and join the chorus, fa la la la la, la la la la.
Follow me in merry measure, fa la la, la la la, la la la.
While I tell of Christmas treasure, fa la la la la, la la la la.

Fast away the old year passes, fa la la la la, la la la la.
Hail the new, you lads and lasses, fa la la la la, la la la la.
Sing we joyous all together, fa la la, la la la, la la la.
Heedless of the wind and weather, fa la la la la, la la la la!

Only 365 Days Until Christmas!

Written by Joanna Spathis

Santa would be home any minute! The elves could do nothing but wait. Some looked out the frosty windows in anticipation. Some paced back and forth, back and forth. And some warmed their toes by the fire and whispered to one another.

"Do you think Kyle will like his train?" the youngest elf asked.

"Of course!" the oldest answered.

"And what about Sophie's house?" the little elf continued. "I heard she moved last week. Do you think Santa found her? Do you think he got the address right?"

The elves all smiled. They knew that, in all his years, Santa had never ever missed a house.

No one remembered which elf was the first to see him. The oldest said he could hear the *jingle, jingle, jingle* of the sleigh a mile away. "Places! Places!" another elf called.

The youngest wee elves lined up by the door. They squirmed and danced with excitement. The older elves ran for Santa's slippers, fluffed the cushions of his favorite chair, and gathered the coziest blankets in the house.

Then the elves were quiet, as quiet as mice. They stood perfectly still and listened. *Pfft!* They heard the soft thud of the giant sleigh land on the snow. They heard Santa thanking each reindeer one by one. And then the elves heard the familiar sound of Santa stomping the snow off his boots on the front porch ... just as Mrs. Claus asked him to do.

The doorknob slowly turned. Santa was home!

"Hooray!" the elves shouted. "Welcome back!"

*A Merry Christmas Calls
for Coke, 1960*

As Santa stepped into the house, his cheeks were as red as his suit, and there were ice crystals hanging from his beard. "Ho! Ho! Ho!" he chuckled and stretched his arms to scoop up as many elves as he could.

"Were there cookies?" asked the youngest elves.

"Of course there were cookies," an older elf answered as he tugged at Santa's heavy coat. "Were they tasty?" he asked.

"The cookies were delicious!" Santa said. "Almost as good as the ones Mrs. Claus bakes."

"What about Evan?" another elf asked. "Was he asleep?"

"Yes," Santa laughed. "He didn't even stir."

The elves were satisfied.

"Tomorrow, children all over the world will wake up to toys under their Christmas trees," Santa said. "You've made a lot of children happy, and you've made me very proud."

"This year I'm going to make a bicycle for Evelyn!" a young elf said eagerly. "It's going to be green."

Santa patted the elf's head. "She will love it."

"And I'm going to start working on a new game for Owen and a dollhouse for his sister Nora."

"And I..."

"Ho! Ho! Hold on a minute!" Santa said with a smile. "Don't we all deserve a moment to pause and refresh?"

"Of course!" the elves shouted.

And so that's what they did. The elves gathered around Santa as he warmed his toes. They fell asleep listening to stories of his busy night. Santa and his elves needed their rest; tomorrow would be a busy day. After all, Christmas was only 365 days away.

Santa's Pause, 1958

Happy Christmas to all,
and to all a good night!

Untitled, 1966